Visual Geography Series®

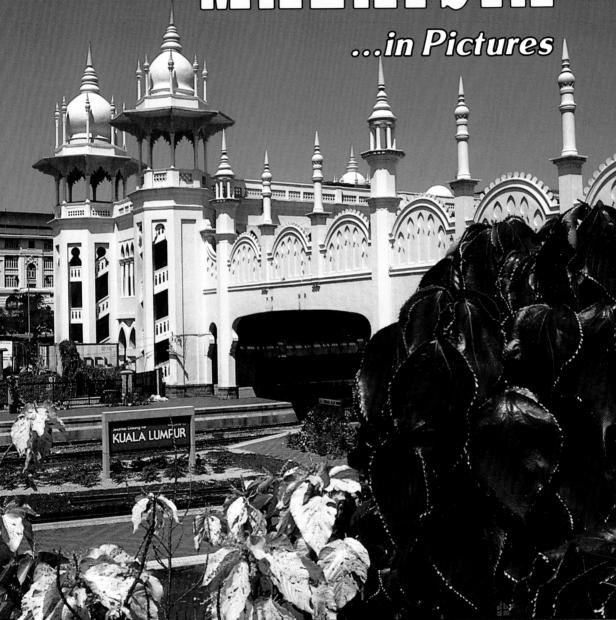

MALAYSIA

...in Pictures

KUALA LUMPUR

Prepared by
Geography Department

Lerner Publications Company
Minneapolis

Independent Picture Service

A Malaysian family winnows rice, letting the wind blow the lighter dust and chaff away from the grain.

This is an all-new edition of the Visual Geography Series. Previous editions have been published by Sterling Publishing Company, New York City, and some of the original textual information has been retained. New photographs, maps, charts, captions, and updated information have been added. The text has been entirely reset in 10/12 Century Textbook.

LIBRARY OF CONGRESS CATALOGING-IN-PUBLICATION DATA

Malaysia in pictures / prepared by Geography Department.

p. cm. — (Visual geography series)
Includes index.
Summary: Malaysia's topography, history, society, economy, and government are concisely described, augmented by photographs, maps, charts, and captions.
ISBN 0-8225-1854-6
1. Malaysia. [1. Malaysia.] I. Lerner Publications Company, Geography Dept. II. Series: Visual geography series (Minneapolis, Minn.)
DS592.M346 1989   88–15887
959.5—dc19   CIP
                                     AC

International Standard Book Number: 0-8225-1854-6
Library of Congress Catalog Card Number: 88-15887

VISUAL GEOGRAPHY SERIES®

Publisher
Harry Jonas Lerner
Associate Publisher
Nancy M. Campbell
Senior Editor
Mary M. Rodgers
Editor
Gretchen Bratvold
Assistant Editors
Dan Filbin
Kathleen S. Heidel
Illustrations Editor
Karen A. Sirvaitis
Consultants/Contributors
L. J. Zwier
Sandra K. Davis
Designer
Jim Simondet
Cartographer
Carol F. Barrett
Indexer
Kristine S. Schubert
Production Manager
Richard J. Hannah

Independent Picture Service

Ornate costumes enhance traditional Chinese operas, which are performed in most Malaysian cities.

Acknowledgments

Title page photo courtesy of L. J. Zwier.

Elevation contours adapted from *The Times Atlas of the World*, seventh comprehensive edition (New York: Times Books, 1985).

1 2 3 4 5 6 7 8 9 10 98 97 96 95 94 93 92 91 90 89

Formalized combat rituals symbolize centuries of Malay history. Such dance forms encourage cultural identity and unity among Malays.

Contents

Introduction **5**

1) The Land **8**
  Topography. Bodies of Water. Climate. Flora. Fauna. Cities.

2) History and Government **20**
  Early Influences. The Rise of Malacca. European Interest. Borneo's Links with the Penin-
  sula. Sarawak and James Brooke. Sabah's Colonial Origin. Britain and the Peninsula.
  Early Twentieth Century. The Japanese Occupation. The Aftermath of World War II.
  The Emergency. Independence. Boundary Debates. Trouble with Neighbors. Ethnic
  Relations and the 1969 Riots. The Aftermath of the Riots. The 1980s. Governmental
  Structure.

3) The People **42**
  Ethnic Mixture. Other Ethnic Groups. Religion. Language. Education. The Arts. Health.
  Sports.

4) The Economy **55**
  Petroleum. Forestry. Mining. Agriculture. Industry. Transportation and Energy. Tourism.
  Future Challenges.

Index **64**

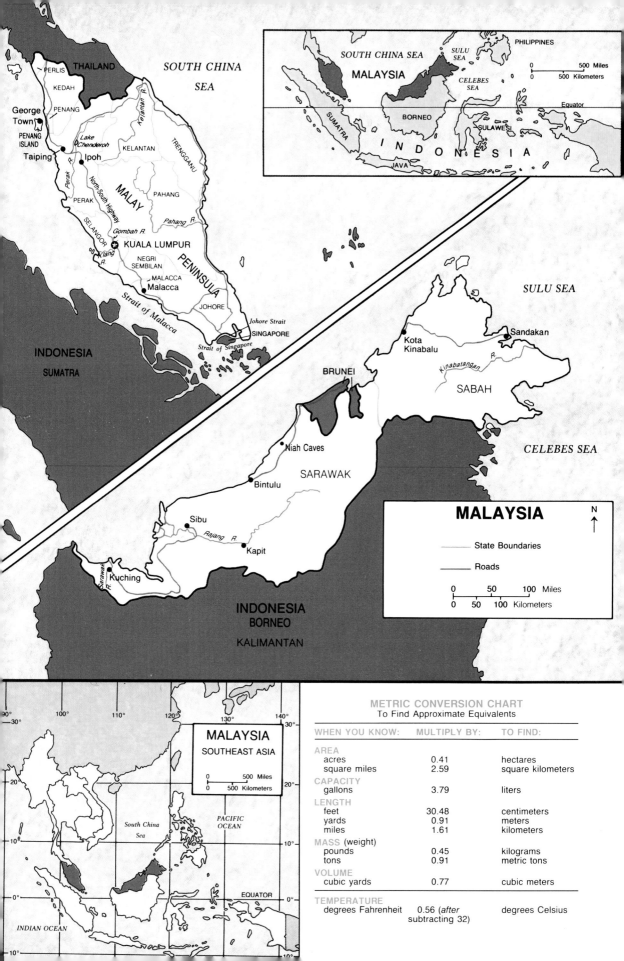

Inset map (top right)

PHILIPPINES

SOUTH CHINA SEA

SULU SEA

MALAYSIA

CELEBES SEA

500 Miles

500 Kilometers

SUMATRA

BORNEO

SULAWESI

I N D O N E S I A

JAVA

Equator

Main map

THAILAND

SOUTH CHINA SEA

PERLIS

KEDAH

PENANG

George Town

PENANG ISLAND

Taiping

Lake Chenderoh

Ipoh

KELANTAN

Kelantan R.

TRENGGANU

Perak R.

PERAK

North-South Highway

MALAY

PAHANG

Pahang R.

SELANGOR

Gombah R.

KUALA LUMPUR

Klang R.

NEGRI SEMBILAN

MALACCA

Malacca

PENINSULA

JOHORE

Strait of Malacca

Johore Strait

SINGAPORE

Strait of Singapore

INDONESIA

SUMATRA

SULU SEA

Kota Kinabalu

Sandakan

Kinabatangan R.

SABAH

BRUNEI

CELEBES SEA

Niah Caves

SARAWAK

Bintulu

Sibu

Rajang R.

Kapit

Sarawak R.

Kuching

INDONESIA

BORNEO

KALIMANTAN

Legend

MALAYSIA

N

State Boundaries

Roads

0   50   100 Miles

0   50   100 Kilometers

Bottom-left map

90° 100° 110° 120° 130° 140°

30°

MALAYSIA

SOUTHEAST ASIA

500 Miles

500 Kilometers

20°

South China Sea

PACIFIC OCEAN

10°

0° EQUATOR

INDIAN OCEAN

10°

Metric Conversion Chart

METRIC CONVERSION CHART
To Find Approximate Equivalents

WHEN YOU KNOW:	MULTIPLY BY:	TO FIND:
AREA		
acres	0.41	hectares
square miles	2.59	square kilometers
CAPACITY		
gallons	3.79	liters
LENGTH		
feet	30.48	centimeters
yards	0.91	meters
miles	1.61	kilometers
MASS (weight)		
pounds	0.45	kilograms
tons	0.91	metric tons
VOLUME		
cubic yards	0.77	cubic meters
TEMPERATURE		
degrees Fahrenheit	0.56 (*after* subtracting 32)	degrees Celsius

On the horizon, across part of the South China Sea, lies Trengganu. This state is located on the eastern coast of Malaysia.

Introduction

An independent nation since 1963, Malaysia has achieved a level of prosperity and freedom that is unusual among Southeast Asian countries. Unlike many other Asian states, Malaysia has avoided difficulties such as too many people, too few resources, harsh or ineffective governments, and widespread poverty. The average Malaysian citizen enjoys a standard of living that is higher than that of any other Asian nation except Japan and Singapore.

Malaysia is composed of two pieces of Southeast Asian territory that lie 400 miles from each other in the South China Sea. One section is the end of the long Malay Peninsula, and the other is made up of the northern coast of the large island of Borneo. Although the two regions have

Godowns (warehouses) line the waterfront at George Town, capital of the island state of Penang, which lies off Peninsular Malaysia's western coast.

distinct histories, they both contributed to the trade between China and India that probably began around the second century A.D. The regions also share a history of British colonial rule.

Many Chinese and Indian immigrants came to the area after the early trade began, and they are now involved in a significant part of Malaysia's economy. Many Chinese and Indian businesspeople grew wealthy as the territories' tin and rubber industries flourished during the nineteenth and early twentieth centuries. Partly because of their economic success, these minorities are often in conflict with the majority Malaysian group—called Malays —whose ancestry stems directly from the peninsular region.

Malays—seeking to establish themselves as economic equals—have responded by giving themselves special privileges under the law. The great differences in wealth on the one hand and legal privileges on the other have created tensions among Malaysia's ethnic groups.

Malaysia encountered both political and economic challenges as it emerged into nationhood. In 1960, on the eve of achieving independence, Malaysia finally defeated a Communist takeover attempt that had begun in 1948. In the early 1960s Malaysia also fended off acts of war by Indonesia and threats from the Philippines. Large profits from the international trade of Malaysian products gained the country peace and prosperity during the 1970s and early 1980s. But the mid-1980s brought lower prices for the country's exports, which caused an economic slowdown.

Malaysia also faces other internal difficulties. Corrupt government officials hurt the economy and discourage foreign investors. Restrictions on what Malaysian newspapers may print and on what the people may discuss in public have limited their right to express themselves.

Yet most Malaysians feel that their troubles are only temporary. With their natural resources and their tradition of free elections, Malaysians believe they have the tools to overcome the nation's current difficulties.

Villagers in Sabah listen to a United Nations representative just prior to the establishment of the Federation of Malaysia. Sabah became part of the federation in September 1963.

Orchids abound in Malaysia, often in unexpected places. Many of the approximately 800 orchid species are epiphytes (air plants) that grow on the branches of trees and get nutrients and moisture from the air. Others sprout in rotting tree stumps.

Courtesy of Tourist Development Corporation of Malaysia

1) The Land

The Federation of Malaysia lies just north of the equator in Southeast Asia. One part of Malaysia contains 11 states and occupies the southern third of the narrow Malay Peninsula, including many nearby islands. Two additional states, Sarawak and Sabah, form the other portion of Malaysia and take up most of the northern coast of the large island of Borneo. At their nearest point, Borneo and Peninsular Malaysia are about 400 miles from each other.

Peninsular Malaysia borders Thailand in the north, and the island nation of Singapore lies just across the Johore Strait in the south. Sarawak and Sabah share the island of Borneo with Kalimantan, an Indonesian province that forms the southern border of these states. Sarawak also shares a frontier with the coastal nation of Brunei.

The total area of Malaysia is 127,580 square miles, making the nation a little larger than the state of New Mexico. Peninsular Malaysia accounts for about 40 percent of the country's total area and stretches for a distance of about 460 miles from north to south. At its widest point, Peninsular Malaysia is slightly over 200 miles in width. The Bornean states of Sarawak and Sabah contain about 60 percent of Malaysia's land area, extending approximately 700 miles in length from the west end of Sarawak to the easternmost point of Sabah.

Topography

A single series of mountains composed of several different ranges dominates the topography of both portions of Malaysia. This chain begins in Burma, continues to the tip of Peninsular Malaysia, dips under the South China Sea, and reappears on the island of Borneo. The mountains consist of granite ridges that arose millions of years ago when the earth's crust pushed

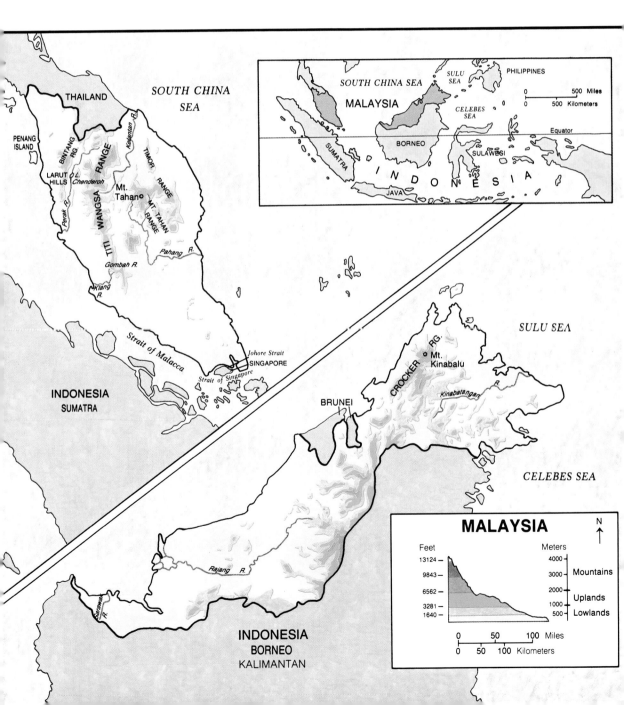

The wave action of the South China Sea creates white, sandy beaches on the eastern coast of Peninsular Malaysia. Fishermen have just unloaded the morning's catch from these boats.

upwards and folded onto itself. The coastal plains that surround these regions are narrow and often swampy, eventually giving way to the lush rain-forests that grow on the mountainsides.

Despite the greenness of its vegetation, Malaysia does not have very fertile land. The heat and monsoon rains rob the soil of many of its nutrients, making it more suitable for specialized export crops (such as rubber and palm oil) than for growing vegetables or grains.

PENINSULAR MALAYSIA

Four major mountain ranges exist in Peninsular Malaysia. In the west the Bintang Range—a short spur of mountains—runs southward from the border of Thailand to the Larut Hills near the Malaysian city of Taiping. Just east of the Bintang Range is the Titi Wangsa Range, which is the longest stretch of high country in Peninsular Malaysia. Titi Wangsa's peaks extend along more than half the length of this portion of the peninsula. Visible from the capital city of Kuala Lumpur and other population centers in western Malaysia, this range contains many summits that reach heights of 6,000 feet above sea level.

A third chain, the Mount Tahan Range, rises in the central region and runs southeast almost to the Pahang River Valley. At that point the mountains level out into a series of highland plains that continue to the southern end of the peninsula. The range takes its name from Mount Tahan, which at 7,175 feet is Peninsular Malaysia's highest peak. The Timor Range is the easternmost of the four mountain chains, and it runs along the upper two-thirds of Malaysia's peninsula. Its highest peaks lie about 50 miles from the South China Sea.

Coastal plains flank the mountainous interior of Peninsular Malaysia. Mangrove swamps and mud flats fringe the western coastal plain, which is 50 miles wide in most places. This region also supports the largest population and the greatest economic activity. The narrower eastern coastal plain consists of broad, sandy beaches formed by the pounding of the rough South China Sea.

Malaysia's mountains are folded granite ridges that are part of a single chain stretching from Burma to Borneo.

Courtesy of Malaysia Tourist Information Center

SARAWAK AND SABAH

The great mountain chain that sinks underneath the sea at the tip of the peninsula resurfaces on the island of Borneo as a group of mountain ranges that run from west to east. In extreme western Sarawak these mountains—which rarely exceed 5,000 feet—rise close to the seacoast. Through most of Sarawak the mountains begin some 60 miles inland from the coast. The most spectacular of Borneo's mountain chains, the Crocker Range rises in western Sabah and extends northeast.

Near the eastern end of this range stands Mount Kinabalu (13,698 feet), the highest peak in Asia southeast of the Himalayas.

Although the plain between Borneo's mountains and its northern coast is often narrow, some portions of it reach 50 miles in width, especially in central Sarawak. Estuaries (where ocean tides meet river currents) deeply indent Sarawak's coast, which is generally swampy. The eastern coast of Sabah, on the Sulu and Celebes seas, is also very irregular and is marked by a number of bays.

Independent Picture Service

In the distance, Mount Kinabalu rises to an altitude of 13,698 feet on the northern coast of Borneo. The peak is part of the Crocker Range and contrasts sharply with the flat rice fields of Sabah that flourish in the lowlands.

11

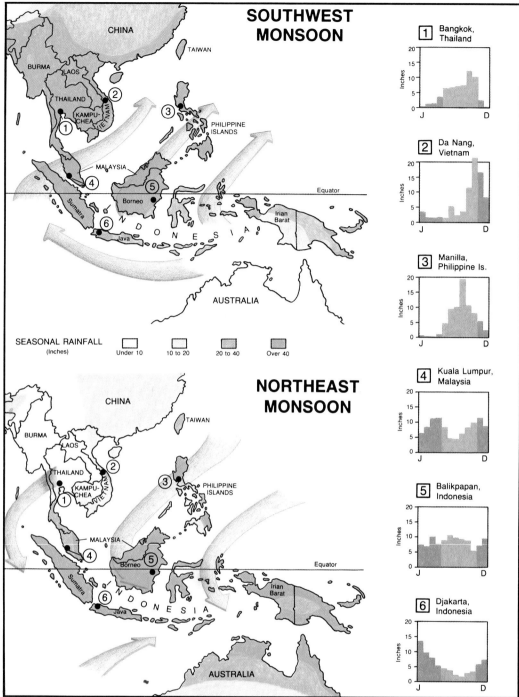

SEASONAL RAINFALL (Inches): Under 10 | 10 to 20 | 20 to 40 | Over 40

Artwork by Carol F. Barrett

These maps show the seasonal shift of winds, called monsoons, over Southeast Asia and the rainfall levels for six cities in the region. From May to October, the winds blow from the southwest. From November to April, they come from the northeast. Because the monsoons in Southeast Asia travel over the ocean, they bring rain to coastal and island areas. The southwest monsoon carries rain to Southeast Asia and to islands north of the equator. These areas are dry during the northeast monsoon period. Islands south of the equator receive moisture from the northeast monsoon but are relatively dry during the southwest monsoon period. Both monsoons bring rain to islands on the equator. Lying fairly near the equator, Kuala Lumpur, Malaysia, gets substantial rainfall throughout the year. Sizable amounts fall in April as a result of the *sumatran*, a local weather pattern that forms off the coast of Peninsular Malaysia. The smallest quantities of rain are received during June, July, and August – the height of the southwest monsoon season. Data taken from *World-Climates* by Willy Rudloff, Stuttgart, 1981.

Bodies of Water

Many rivers and streams—the result of the country's year-round rains—cross Malaysia. The longest rivers—the Rajang and the Kinabatangan—flow through Sarawak and Sabah respectively. Both rivers traverse 350 miles, providing valuable routes for trade and communication in interior regions, where few roads exist. Oceangoing freighters navigate the first 40 miles of the Rajang to the town of Sibu, and coastal steamers continue upstream another 60 miles to Kapit.

In the mountains, the rivers in Sarawak and Sabah flow straight and quickly, but they move slowly through the coastal plains. Sediments carried by the water often collect at the mouths of these rivers, forming swampy deltas where mangrove forests develop.

In Peninsular Malaysia, the longest waterway is the 205-mile-long Pahang, which flows east into the South China Sea. The Kelantan River also empties into the South China Sea, and another major river, the Perak, runs into the Strait of Malacca, which lies between Malaysia and Indonesia. Many Malay villages—called kampongs—lie along the banks of the peninsula's waterways, which provide both a means of transportation as well as fishing areas for the residents.

Very few lakes of any great size exist in Malaysia. The largest, Lake Chenderoh, is artificial and was formed when the Perak River was dammed to create a hydroelectric plant.

Climate

Because Malaysia is located in the tropics, the amount of sunlight that reaches the country is constant throughout the year. As a result, very little change occurs in the average daily temperature from month to month. Daytime highs are usually in the upper eighties or low nineties, and nighttime lows are usually in the mid-seventies. The highest temperature ever recorded in

Photo by L. J. Zwier

Robinson Falls tumble over a granite outcropping in the lush forests of the Cameron Highlands, which lie in Peninsular Malaysia.

Peninsular Malaysia was 102° F, and the lowest recorded temperature—taken in the Titi Wangsa Mountains—was 36° F.

Although daily humidity levels hover around 85 percent and temperatures are high, Malaysia's climate is not always uncomfortable. Two factors—altitude and cloud cover—moderate the temperatures. In Malaysia's high country, days range from slightly cool to pleasantly warm, and nights are chilly enough to make jackets and warm blankets necessary.

Malaysia's two monsoon seasons—from November to April and from May to October—also affect temperatures. A monsoon is a seasonal wind that usually blows across a large expanse of ocean and gathers water vapor, which is deposited as rain. Another weather pattern called a *sumatran* appears on the western coast of Peninsular Malaysia in April. Sumatrans form over the Strait of Malacca during the night and move ashore at various times of the day, bringing heavy rain and high winds.

The eastern coast of Malaysia receives very heavy rain during the monsoons in December and January, and flooding is frequent. The rainiest place in Peninsular Malaysia, however, is on the western coast near the city of Taiping, where the average annual rainfall is 232 inches. Kuala Lumpur receives about 85 inches of rain in an average year, the city of Kuching in Sarawak gets about 162 inches, and Kota Kinabalu in Sabah receives about 94 inches.

Flora

Malaysia's tropical climate and abundant rainfall support thick and varied vegetation. Tropical forests cover about 78,000 square miles—60 percent—of Malaysia. Scientists have identified about 3,000 species of trees in these forests, and still more have yet to be cataloged. Malaysia's forests consist primarily of hardwood trees, although a few stands of pine grow in the hills. Palm trees usually appear near rivers or villages, where the competition for sunlight is not as fierce as it is in the thick forests.

Photo by L. J. Zwier

Beyond the narrow blue strait that appears through the trees lies heavily wooded Kapas Island, just east of Peninsular Malaysia in the South China Sea.

The tree in the center carries the tendrils (stems) of a climbing vine, which supports the spreading leaves of other jungle plants.

Photo by J. M. Zwier

The forests have sparse vegetation at ground level because the branches of tall trees form a leafy canopy that allows little light to filter through to smaller species. Thick vines called lianas take root on the floor of the rain-forest and climb the large trees to find sunlight in the upper reaches of the forest. Other plants called epiphytes, or air plants, find rootholds on upper tree branches and then send down slender supporting stems that gather moisture directly from the humid air.

15

The *bunga raya* (great flower), a variety of hibiscus, is both beautiful and useful. Medicinal teas are made from it, and the red petals yield a dye. The bunga raya is Malaysia's national flower, and in 1967 it replaced the symbol for Singapore on the country's coat of arms.

Photo by J. M. Zwier

Fauna

A variety of wild animals, such as tigers and elephants, still inhabit the jungles of Peninsular Malaysia. Other large mammals of the Malaysian jungles include a small number of rhinoceroses and leopards that occur both on the peninsula and on Borneo. The tapir (a large, hoofed animal related to the horse and rhinoceros) is common on the peninsula, as are wild pigs, otters, civet cats, deer, and bears. Monkeys are an ordinary sight, even near cities, and rare orangutans live in some parts of the Bornean jungles.

Courtesy of Tourist Development Corporation of Malaysia

People have hunted Malaysia's orangutans, intelligent and nonaggressive apes, until they have been nearly eliminated from their home territories in Sabah, Sarawak, and on the nearby Indonesian island of Sumatra.

The tapir often appears to be just another shapeless splash of light when it travels through the jungle, with its black forequarters and hind legs hidden in the shadows. This mild plant-eater weighs up to 1,000 pounds and can stay underwater for long periods to escape its enemies.

Monitor lizards scavenge for both animals and plants and can grow up to eight feet long. The largest lizards in Malaysia, monitors are closely related to the Komodo dragons of Indonesia, the largest lizards on earth.

Large crocodiles are common in Malaysian rivers, and the country is home to over 100 species of snakes, although most are not poisonous. Dangerous snakes include king cobras, Wagler's pit vipers, and the Malaysian python—one of the world's largest snakes. Malaysia also features over 500 varieties of birds and many kinds of butterflies.

The rhinoceros hornbill of Sarawak is usually about four feet long, and its bony nosepiece makes it unmistakable among Borneo's many bird species.

17

Since 1896, when it was declared the administrative capital of the British-controlled Federated Malay States, Kuala Lumpur has shed its image as a mining town. The city's businesses handle much of the world's trade in rubber, tin, and palm oil.

Cities

Although most Malaysians live in small villages, the country has several large cities, including Kuala Lumpur (population 1.1 million), the nation's capital. Lying on the western side of Peninsular Malaysia, Kuala Lumpur is situated where the Klang and the Gombah rivers meet. This location gave the city its name, which means "muddy river junction" in the Malay language. Built in the mid-nineteenth century as a tin-mining town, Kuala Lumpur is now the commercial center of Malaysia.

George Town (population 325,000) is a trading center on Penang Island, just off Peninsular Malaysia's western coast. The British established the settlement as a naval base in 1786, and the city has encouraged trade over the years by becoming a free port (where goods shipped in and out of the country are not taxed). Ipoh (population 500,000), a center for tin mining, also lies on Peninsular Malaysia's heavily populated western side. This city is named after the ipoh tree, whose sap Malay people once used as poison on their hunting darts.

A center of trade and the state capital of Sarawak, Kuching (population 230,000) lies 10 miles inland from the coast. The Sarawak River divides the city into residential and commercial districts. Sibu (population 50,000) is Sarawak's other major city. Lying about 40 miles inland on the Rajang River, Sibu is a port for much of the commercial activity along the river.

A port on the South China Sea, Kota Kinabalu (population 130,000) is Sabah's capital. On the coast of the Sulu Sea, Sandakan (population 118,000) has a large harbor that handles eastern Sabah's commercial trade.

Photo by Bernice K. Condit

Kuala Lumpur – Malay words meaning "muddy river junction" – is located where the Klang and Gombah rivers come together.

Photo by L. J. Zwier

Kuching, the capital of Sarawak, is built on both banks of the Sarawak River. Instead of being connected by a bridge, the city uses small ferries to transport people and goods across the river.

Marchers carry the Malaysian flag as they parade in celebration of National Day every August 31. Tunku Abdul Rahman, the nation's founder, proclaimed the country's independence on that date in 1957.

2) History and Government

In the course of Malaysian history, peoples from many parts of the world have left their mark on the region. Some came as conquerors, others as settlers. In Sarawak, archaeological discoveries at the Niah Caves show that humans lived in the region as long ago as 50,000 B.C. Archaeologists think that the earliest inhabitants of Malaysia were similar to ethnic groups that still live in caves and that hunt wild animals in parts of New Guinea and the Philippines.

This early Stone Age population lived undisturbed in the jungles of Malaysia un-til about 2000 B.C., when late Stone Age people, who had more complex stone tools, moved into Malaysia. The newcomers, known as Proto-Malays (*proto* means "first"), probably originated in what is now southwestern China. The Proto-Malays had a more developed culture than the original Malay inhabitants, who were either driven out of the region or left to populate the more remote parts of Malaysia.

Another wave of immigrants reached Malaysia about 250 B.C. and brought with them knowledge of how to make metal tools. The origin of these newcomers is uncertain, but ancient chants that are attributed to them have features of the Sanskrit language—a classical Indian tongue. Other evidence—especially found in place-names, such as Sungei Melay (Malay River), which are still used in Sumatra —links them to southeastern Sumatra.

Early Influences

Since prehistoric times, the two giants of the Asian continent—India and China— have influenced Southeast Asia. Indian merchants opened trading posts along the shores of what are now Malaysia and Indonesia, and Malay seafarers traveled to India. As a result of these commercial exchanges, the Malay people began to absorb India's cultural heritage.

Beginning in the second century A.D., Indian merchants developed trading centers along the western coast of the peninsula. Over the centuries, these kampongs came under the control of several foreign kingdoms. For example, at the beginning of the seventh century Buddhism (a religious faith inspired by Gautama Buddha in the

Indian traders brought the Hindu religion to Malaysia as they began exchanging goods with Malays in the late first century A.D. A Hindu temple is decorated with statues of gods on each of its tiers.

The second emperor of the Chinese Tang dynasty, Tai Zong, ruled from A.D. 626 to 649. He continued to tax the small empires, including those in Peninsular Malaysia, that lined the trade routes controlled by China.

National Palace Museum, Taiwan

fifth century B.C.) spread toward the Malay Peninsula. The powerful Buddhist kingdom of Sri Vijaya that arose on the island of Sumatra soon extended its influence over the Malay Peninsula.

Sri Vijayan rule, however, was not unopposed, and attacks on the kingdom's hold- ings began as early as A.D. 992. In time the balance of power shifted to the Javanese kingdom of Majapahit and to the Thai kingdom of Sukhothai.

Since the sixth century A.D., China had demanded that tribute (payments) and trade from the small empires in the region come directly to China. By the end of the twelfth century, however, Chinese merchants began making trading voyages of their own. Some Chinese began to live permanently in the region of Peninsular Malaysia during this period, and their settlements became the foundation for the future growth of Chinese commercial power in Malaysia's cities and towns.

The Rise of Malacca

In 1402 Paramesvara, a refugee prince from Sumatra, murdered the ruler of Tumasik (a territory later to become Singapore) and seized control of the region. The invader fled when a Thai army approached to regain control of the area. Paramesvara made his way up the Malay Peninsula to the western coastal village of Malacca, a small settlement of Malay pirates and fishermen. He soon built Malacca into a thriving port by attracting traders, more pirates, and other Malays to settle there. Paramesvara ensured the security of the trading center by negotiating with China's strong Ming dynasty to protect Malacca.

Those who ruled Malacca after Paramesvara expanded trade throughout the region, and Malaccan rulers extended their realm to include a large portion of surrounding land. In 1445 Muzaffar Shah, a local Malay leader, became ruler of Malacca and decreed Islam to be the territory's official religion. This monotheistic (one-god) religion had been founded on the Arabian Peninsula by the seventh-century prophet Muhammad.

Although Arab and Indian Muslims (followers of Islam) had brought Islam to the area long ago, nearby Buddhist and Hindu empires had limited the expansion of Islam. (Hinduism had been the dominant religion of India since about 1500 B.C.) But

Courtesy of Northwest Orient

Since the fifteenth century, when Muzaffar Shah's followers became Muslims, Islam has been an important religion in Malaysia. These domes of a mosque (Islamic place of prayer) are surrounded by minarets (towers) from which the faithful are called to worship.

Muzaffar Shah, taking the title of sultan (a Muslim title of nobility), set in motion the increasingly rapid growth of Islam.

Malacca's success attracted attention from European explorers who had begun to sail across the Indian Ocean in search of spices and wealth. In 1511 a fleet led by Portugal's viceroy in India, Don Alfonso de Albuquerque, appeared in Malacca. The well-armed Portuguese fleet captured the great Malay city after intense fighting. But because the Portuguese were primarily interested in trade, they did not establish a colonial government. Although the Portuguese left the region largely on its own, their presence diminished the strength of the local sultans, who became vulnerable to outside powers.

Santiago Arch is all that remains of a large Portuguese fort that guarded Malacca in the sixteenth century. Strongly built, the fort protected a small garrison of soldiers that the Portuguese stationed on the western coast of Peninsular Malaysia during its period of colonial control.

European Interest

Opportunities for quick profits from the trade of Asian spices introduced to Europeans by the Portuguese soon attracted British and Dutch traders. Spices were in heavy demand in Europe, and a successful voyage could bring a profit that was four times as high as the cost of the entire expedition. To organize commercial activity in Indian and Asian waters, British traders established the British East India Company in 1600, and the Dutch began the United East India Company in 1602.

Portugal's hold on lands in Southeast Asia weakened as the Dutch increased their activity in the area. Although Malacca fell to the Dutch in 1641, the city soon declined in importance because the primary Dutch port on the island of Java absorbed much of Malacca's trade. Although Malacca had been prosperous under the sultans and even under the Portuguese, most Malays gained little from the rich trading center. In general, Malays continued to farm and fish in their kampongs.

The British were the next Europeans to show interest in Malaya, as the region came to be known under British rule. The British East India Company signed an agreement with one of the sultans of the region in 1786. The document allowed the British to settle on Penang Island and to establish a naval station (which eventually became George Town) and trading facilities. In return, the sultan asked for an annual payment and for British protection in case his territory were attacked.

In 1819 Thomas Stamford Raffles from the British East India Company selected the island of Singapore at the very tip of the peninsula as the site for a new trading center. At first a desolate and almost unpopulated island, Singapore became a major seaport under Raffles's guidance.

In 1826 the British East India Company combined Penang, Malacca, and Singapore into a single territory known as the Straits Settlements. The company managed the region's trade from its headquarters in

The Bettmann Archive

In 1819 Thomas Stamford Raffles chose the island of Singapore as the site for a British trading center, which soon became the dominant port throughout the South China Sea.

Independent Picture Service

The British free port at Singapore combined with Penang and Malacca in 1826 to form the Straits Settlements.

India until 1857, when the British government directly began to administer the territory. In 1867—after years of prompting by merchants of Singapore, Penang, and Malacca—the British declared the Straits Settlements to be a colony.

Borneo's Links with the Peninsula

Just as Chinese traders gradually built up communities on the peninsula, they likewise established their presence on Borneo. By the fourteenth century the Chinese had become so involved on the island that Chinese meanings for places became prominent. (Kinabalu, for example, means "Chinese Widow.") Borneo was a trading partner with Peninsular Malaysia during the fifteenth century. Not only did commerce bind the two regions, but intermarriage between their ruling families also united them.

Islam, which spread from Malacca, gained a strong foothold on Borneo, and in the late fifteenth century the Islamic kingdom of Brunei was established on the northern coast. Spain acquired a large portion of the territory of Borneo in the sixteenth century, and the Dutch made a few

Independent Picture Service

The rain-forests of Sabah yield valuable hardwood timber. The British North Borneo Company, which received timber-cutting rights from the region's leaders, gained a foothold in the territory in the 1880s. After World War II, Sabah became a British colony.

contacts from the seventeenth to the nineteenth centuries, mostly in southern Borneo.

Sarawak and James Brooke

In the early nineteenth century most of the northern coast of Borneo was under the sultan of Brunei's leadership. Various pirate chiefs of the Iban and other Bornean ethnic groups constantly threatened the sultan's control over the territory. By the time the British adventurer James Brooke arrived in Borneo in 1839, the sultan's kingdom was in the midst of a rebellion.

The hard-pressed sultan of Brunei accepted Brooke's offer of aid—particularly the firepower of the cannons on Brooke's ship—and the rebellion was quickly put down. In 1841 the sultan granted Brooke the title of raja (prince) of the western section of present-day Sarawak. Brooke established his capital at Kuching and began ruling his private kingdom, for which he paid the sultan a small annual tribute.

In 1868 James Brooke died, and his nephew, Charles Brooke, inherited control of Sarawak. The territory grew as the new

The Bettmann Archive

In a period drawing, James Brooke and the sultan of Brunei negotiate an agreement in 1841. Under the treaty, Brooke's ship would police the waters of Borneo, and in return Brooke would gain control of a large section of Sarawak.

raja purchased land, and soon the sultan of Brunei was left with only two small pieces of territory along the Belait and Temburong rivers.

After reigning for 50 years, Charles Brooke died, and his son Charles Vyner Brooke succeeded him. The third raja promoted self-rule for Sarawak, but World War II hampered his plans. Japanese troops occupied Borneo until the end of the war. In 1946 Charles Vyner Brooke gave the land, which had been his family's private kingdom for more than 100 years, to Great Britain as a colony.

Sabah's Colonial Origin

The territory that is now the Malaysian state of Sabah was much sought after by Western traders during the nineteenth century. Under the sultan of Brunei, local chiefs had controlled the territory, which the sultan of Sulu, in northeastern Borneo, had also claimed. Western merchants made many attempts to sign timber-cutting agreements for the precious hardwoods of the rain-forest with one or both sultans. In 1881 trading rights finally went to the British North Borneo Company, which administered Sabah for the British government. The territory, then known as North Borneo, became a British protectorate in 1888 and a colony after World War II.

Britain and the Peninsula

During the second half of the nineteenth century, large deposits of tin ore were discovered on the western side of the peninsula. Chinese financiers in the Straits Settlements supplied the capital (the original investment of money) to develop tin

Independent Picture Service

This tin mine near Kuala Lumpur still makes use of some of the innovations developed by nineteenth-century Chinese miners.

mines and brought thousands of workers from China. The mineowners often treated the Chinese immigrants badly, and many of the workers died from disease.

The Chinese mine workers organized into competitive secret societies and frequently fought one another. The local Malay rulers added to the tense situation by quarreling over their share of the tax money from the Chinese-owned tin mines.

Demands for a solution to these difficulties came from both British and Chinese commercial leaders of the Straits Settlements. These leaders viewed the bloodshed, violence, and pirate raids along the coasts as bad for business.

In 1874 the governor of the Straits Settlements and Sultan Abdullah, the strongest local leader, signed the Treaty of Pangkor. The British agreed to recognize the sultan's claim to the western Malay Peninsula, and Abdullah agreed to accept the guidance of a British resident adviser on all matters except those concerning the Islamic religion and Malay customs. The treaty made the British the real rulers of the region, and the sultan's role became mainly ceremonial.

The effectiveness of the adviser system depended to a large extent on the tact and understanding of the British official. Some of the Malay leaders killed the first adviser, W. W. Birch, in part because the changes that he introduced lowered their income. Sir Hugh Low, who was appointed the next adviser, introduced changes more slowly.

Other regions of the peninsula also accepted resident officials. The adviser in Perak opened the first railway in that region. Four territories (Perak, Selangor, Negri Sembilan, and Pahang) merged into the Federated Malay States in 1896 to allow more efficient organization. A treaty between Great Britain and Thailand in 1909 brought the northern peninsular states of Perlis, Kedah, Kelantan, and Trengganu under British control.

Independent Picture Service

A worker sprays chemicals to destroy disease-carrying insects. Chinese immigrants were especially prone to infection by tropical diseases as they adjusted to the new climate.

Independent Picture Service

This mosque at the center of Kuala Lumpur illustrates the influence of the Islamic religion in Malaysia.

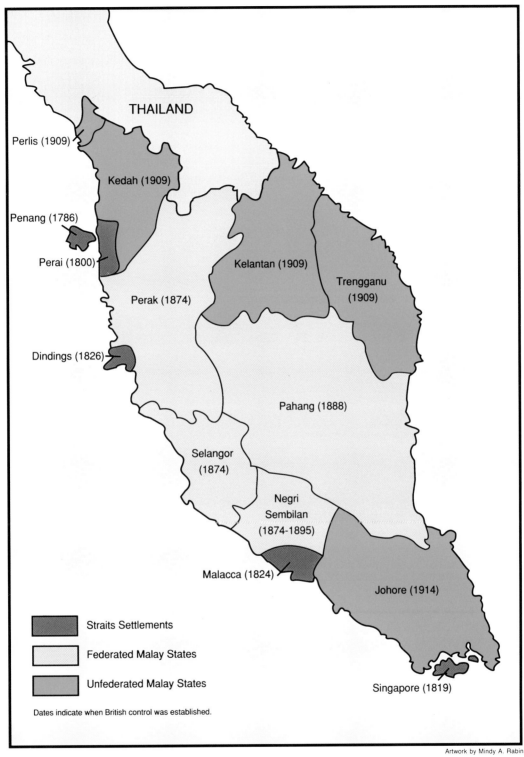

THAILAND

Perlis (1909)

Kedah (1909)

Penang (1786)

Perai (1800)

Perak (1874)

Kelantan (1909)

Trengganu (1909)

Dindings (1826)

Pahang (1888)

Selangor (1874)

Negri Sembilan (1874-1895)

Malacca (1824)

Johore (1914)

Straits Settlements

Federated Malay States

Unfederated Malay States

Dates indicate when British control was established.

Singapore (1819)

Artwork by Mindy A. Rabin

Beginning in 1800, Britain extended its power in Peninsular Malaysia. Its first colony was the Straits Settlements, and Britain later organized other regions into the Federated Malay States. The unfederated states were under Thai control but accepted British protection.

At the beginning of the twentieth century, thousands of Indians emigrated to Malaysia to work on rubber plantations. These workers learned to strip off the tree's bark to tap the plant's sap, called latex.

Independent Picture Service

Early Twentieth Century

A major event in the world's economy at the end of the nineteenth century was a rubber boom, which was fueled by the new global demand for automobile tires. Rubber tree plantations eventually covered 7,500 square miles of land in Peninsular Malaysia. Thousands of workers emigrated from India to work on the rubber plantations, and rubber soon surpassed tin as Malaysia's leading export.

Compared to the rest of Southeast Asia, Peninsular Malaysia was a prosperous and stable place during the first four decades of the twentieth century. With great wealth and a relatively small population, the peninsular states could provide roads, railways, mosquito control, and telephone lines —all of which were rare services in Southeast Asia.

Some Chinese who lived in Peninsular Malaysia grew wealthy, and Indian laborers earned more money on the peninsula than they did in India. Although the Malays had advantages in obtaining political offices, government jobs, and education, they generally did not fare as well economically as foreign workers did. Despite being the largest of the nation's ethnic groups, Malays controlled very few of Malaysia's economic resources. The Chinese owned most shops, factories, mines, and other businesses.

Some Malaysians, especially a number of Chinese, were discontented and became Communist activists, working to establish a system of public ownership of both the land and the means of production. Assisted by organizers from China, the Communists led labor strikes in the 1930s. During the same period, Muslim fundamentalists, who believed in a strict interpretation of religious law, preached that the Western-style system of government introduced by the British was incompatible with Islam.

Despite these agitations, widespread satisfaction among most Malaysians from all ethnic groups created a conservative political climate that discouraged an urgent drive for independence. Before World War II, no significant movement for self-rule emerged in the region of Peninsular Malaysia. Then, on December 8, 1941, the Japanese invasion of the territory began.

The Japanese Occupation

During World War II (1939–1945), the Japanese defeated the British in battles throughout the Malay Peninsula. After their victory in the region in early 1942, the Japanese appointed Malays to many administrative posts. Overall, Malays suffered less from the occupation than the Chinese Malaysians, whom the Japanese persecuted because they had supported China's resistance to the Japanese. This difference in treatment led to post-war tension between Malays and Chinese Malaysians.

Several anti-Japanese resistance movements arose in response to the occupation. The most important groups were the well-organized Communist guerrillas and the Malayan People's Anti-Japanese Army (MPAJA). The British air dropped arms and ammunition to the MPAJA, but the war ended and the Japanese troops withdrew before the organization could use many of the weapons. The MPAJA buried the supplies, saving them for possible future conflict.

The Aftermath of World War II

When the British returned after World War II, important political changes

Photo by L. J. Zwier

A plaque in Malacca honors some of the Malaysian soldiers who died fighting the Japanese in World War II. Malay, Chinese, Indian, Portuguese, and English names show the multiethnic character of the battalion.

Artwork by Jim Simondet

From the end of World War II until the early 1950s, the Federated Malay states used a flag that combined the traditional emblem of Britain with the Malay symbol of a running tiger.

occurred throughout the region. Singapore, Sabah, and Sarawak, for example, became separate British colonies. The Malays wanted to be a majority in whatever nation emerged in Peninsular Malaysia. Malay leaders rejected a British proposal for a Malayan Union because the union would have stripped political power from the Malay sultans. The plan also would have granted citizenship to a large number of non-Malays living on the peninsula—mostly to recent Chinese immigrants.

In 1948 the British established the Federation of Malaya, which kept some local power in the hands of the sultans and which limited non-Malay citizenship. Malays had become a united political group by working together to reject the first British proposal. But the second governmental plan caused great ethnic-based hostility between Malays and non-Malays.

The Emergency

On June 16, 1948, Communist guerrillas entered two rubber estates near Ipoh and killed four British planters. The incident set off a period known as the Emergency. A Communist force numbering 7,000—mostly Chinese led by former members of the MPAJA—unearthed the British arms hidden at the end of World War II. Their civilian supporters—who supplied the jungle fighters with food and other essentials—were few in number. But guerrilla tactics and a frightened population made the Communists a powerful opponent for government troops.

The British helped to defeat the Communists by supplying arms and by solving some of the most pressing rural concerns. The Briggs Plan relocated almost 400,000 poor, landless Chinese from their squatter shacks to new villages where they received

The British built villages for large numbers of Chinese laborers in the 1950s, improving their living conditions in order to make them less likely to support the Communist guerrillas.

Independent Picture Service

Independent Picture Service

During the Emergency, government military vehicles escorted travelers through areas controlled by Communist soldiers.

Government soldiers inspect a car at a checkpoint during the Emergency. The government prohibited people from bringing food and medicine, as well as weaponry, into areas suspected of containing Communist forces.

Independent Picture Service

land, health care, housing, and electricity. The new settlements separated the Chinese population from the Communist guerrillas, and the improved living conditions made these low-income Chinese less likely to support the guerrillas.

British troops who had fought the Japanese in Burma were called in to attack Communist strongholds. By 1958 many guerrilla fighters—including the movement's leader, Chin Peng—had abandoned the fight.

The Emergency ended officially in 1960. The attempted Communist takeover failed in part because few people in Peninsular Malaysia were discontented enough to join the campaign. The tactics of the Communists, including terrorist attacks, turned most Malaysians against them. Calls for independence did not seem necessary because by 1948 the British had already begun the process of granting Malaysian self-rule.

Independence

When it became apparent in the mid-1950s that the Communists had little hope of taking over in Peninsular Malaysia, Great Britain urged the region to become independent. The most prominent political leader in the peninsula at that time was Tunku Abdul Rahman, a prince from the territory of Kedah.

Rahman's party, the United Malays National Organization (UMNO), had joined with the Malayan Chinese Association (MCA) and the Malayan Indian Congress (MIC) to create the Alliance. This multiethnic party won many seats in 1955 during the elections for Malaya's first legislature.

In 1956 a constitutional convention drew up the terms under which the new legislature would function. Finally, on August 31, 1957, the Federation of Malaya achieved *merdeka* (independence), and Tunku Abdul Rahman became the new nation's first prime minister. In framing the

Courtesy of Tourist Development Corporation of Malaysia

These flag bearers guide the National Day march through Kuala Lumpur's National Stadium.

constitution, leaders of the major ethnic groups—Malays, Chinese, and Indians—agreed to a system of special privileges for Malays to offset their economic deficiencies. To help boost Malay economic development, the 1957 constitution gave Malays preference for some scholarships, loans, business permits, and government jobs.

Boundary Debates

Over the next eight years, Malaysians debated about where to draw the boundaries of the new nation. In 1957 the federation included only the 11 states of Peninsular Malaysia—not Singapore, Sarawak, or Sabah. Singapore was a separate British colony, but proposals for it to unite with Malaya were often put forward. Most Malays opposed such a union because Singapore's largely Chinese population would make the Malays a minority in the federation.

To overcome this opposition, Tunku Abdul Rahman and Singapore's chief minister, Lee Kuan Yew, proposed that the other British territories in the region—Sarawak, Brunei, and Sabah—also join. The large number of Iban, Kadazan, and other ethnic groups of these states would keep the Chinese from becoming the majority.

After much campaigning, Singapore, Sarawak, and Sabah voted to join the new nation. These states became part of the newly named independent Federation of Malaysia on September 16, 1963. Brunei decided not to join the union.

The original peoples of Sarawak and Sabah—including the Iban, the Kadazan, and dozens of smaller ethnic groups—received the same privileges that Malays enjoyed. The result was that Malaysian society was split into *bumiputras* (people of the soil), who receive special privileges, and *non-bumiputras*, who do not. Any Malaysian citizen belonging to an ethnic group that lived in the territory before Indian and Chinese immigration began and before the

Courtesy of Tourist Development Corporation of Malaysia

Malaysian Muslims (followers of Islam) gather for an Islamic celebration. All Malays are Muslims, and since independence they have enjoyed special economic privileges in Malaysia.

Courtesy of UNICEF

This Iban father is helping his son dress in ceremonial clothes. The Iban are a major *bumiputra* ethnic group from Sarawak, and they are among those groups that benefit from governmental rights that are withheld from Chinese and Indian ethnic communities.

35

Independent Picture Service

Tunku Abdul Rahman was the first prime minister of Malaysia. A lawyer by training, he is regarded as the nation's founder.

era of European colonization is considered a bumiputra. In essence, bumiputras are the Malays, the Bornean peoples, and the other original groups of the peninsular jungles. A nonbumiputra is any other Malaysian—especially the many Chinese and Indian citizens—who together constitute just under 50 percent of the population.

Lee Kuan Yew disturbed many Malay citizens on the peninsula when he challenged the special governmental privileges that Malays and other bumiputras received. Lee pushed for a "Malaysian Malaysia," in which all citizens would have equal rights regardless of their ethnic background. But Malays feared that without their special privileges, most of the economic power in the federation would remain in Chinese hands. On August 9, 1965, after many meetings between Tunku Abdul Rahman and Lee Kuan Yew, Singapore withdrew from the Federation of Malaysia.

Trouble with Neighbors

In 1963 the Federation of Malaysia nearly went to war with one of its closest neigh-

bors, the Republic of Indonesia. After the federation was announced on September 16, mobs of Indonesians attacked the Malaysian and British embassies in Jakarta, Indonesia's capital. The motive for the attacks was Indonesia's claim to federation territory (especially in Sarawak and Sabah).

In the weeks that followed, Indonesian troops crossed the border into Sarawak, and a few landed on the peninsula and in Singapore, but Malaysia survived the attacks. Soon after Sukarno, Indonesia's president, left office in 1965, Malaysia and Indonesia entered into a peace treaty.

Another neighbor, the Philippines, also opposed the formation of Malaysia, claiming that Sabah was part of Philippine territory. The dispute interrupted diplomatic relations between the two countries several times in the 1960s. Tension has eased in recent years, and a Philippine movement to give up the claim to Sabah is progressing in the Philippine legislature.

Ethnic Relations and the 1969 Riots

In the 1960s, conflicts arose between bumiputras and nonbumiputras over the

Independent Picture Service

Lee Kuan Yew, prime minister of Singapore, negotiated Singapore's entry into Malaysia in 1963, as well as its withdrawal from the country in 1965.

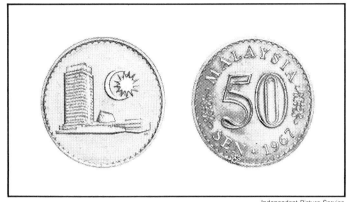

This Malaysian 50-sen coin was minted in 1967 and on one side bears an image of Parliament House in Kuala Lumpur, along with the Islamic symbol of a star and crescent.

system of privileges. By 1969 many non-bumiputras had become very resentful of the privilege system. Much of this resentment focused on their political leaders in the Alliance party who had given away nonbumiputra rights. On the other side, many Malays were also dissatisfied with the Alliance because they thought it had not done enough to win special treatment for Malays.

In the elections for Parliament held on May 10, 1969, opposition parties won many seats previously filled by the Alliance. Because the Alliance controlled fewer than half the seats in Parliament, it disbanded a few days later. Large crowds of Chinese marched in the streets of Kuala Lumpur in celebration of their electoral victory. Street fighting between the Chinese, the Indians, and the Malays broke out in the capital and continued for about two weeks. When the riots were over, several hundred Malaysians—mostly Chinese and Indians —had been killed. The prime minister dissolved Parliament, and a special ruling council assumed control of the government.

The Aftermath of the Riots

The interethnic riots in Kuala Lumpur shocked Malaysians from every ethnic group. Tunku Abdul Rahman, whom the

The ceremonial opening of the Federation of Malaya Parliament in the late 1950s blended British and Malay customs, with a guard in Malay attire leading officials in British dress.

Malays saw as too sympathetic to the concerns of nonbumiputras, resigned in 1970. Tun Abdul Razak, the head of the special ruling council, replaced him as prime minister. The council outlawed public criticism of bumiputra privileges, a prohibition that was still in effect in the late 1980s.

Parliament reopened again in 1971. A broad group of political parties, known as the Barisan Nasional (National Front), came to power. The Barisan Nasional was made up of the original core of the Alliance—the UMNO, the MCA, and the MIC—but many smaller parties joined as well, including the Parti Islam Se-Malaysia (PAS), a Muslim fundamentalist group.

In 1971 the government introduced the New Economic Policy (NEP), a program of legislation that further increased the status of bumiputras. The NEP's most ambitious goal was to give bumiputras control over 30 percent of Malaysia's economic resources by 1990. The government planned to continue the NEP only until 1990. In 1987 about 18 percent of Malaysia's corporate wealth was in the hands of bumiputras—far from the NEP's 30 percent goal.

The 1980s

Datuk Sri Dr. Mahathir Mohamad became Malaysia's prime minister in 1981. Under Mahathir, the nation began to attack illegal drug traffic. Malaysia's mandatory death sentence for those dealing in illegal drugs has led to the execution of many drug dealers—including many foreigners.

Islamic fundamentalism has grown stronger in Malaysia during the 1970s and the 1980s. The Mahathir government has opposed the extreme demands of some Muslims—such as enforcing Islamic law (called sharia) on non-Muslims.

In 1969 riots erupted between Malaysia's ethnic groups. Many Malay and Chinese residents of Kuala Lumpur returned to their homes only to find them burned and damaged as a result of a week of uncontrolled violence.

The flag of Malaysia has seven red and seven white stripes, one for each of the states and one for the federal zone that contains Kuala Lumpur. In the corner on a blue field lies the golden star and crescent—symbols of the Islamic religion.

Artwork by Jim Simondet

Nevertheless, the administration has encouraged a gradual increase of Islamic practices in Malaysian society and has helped Anwar Ibrahim, a Muslim fundamentalist leader, rise in government ranks. Reappointed as minister of education in 1987, Anwar has won support for Mahathir among conservative Muslims. His position of power causes many non-Muslims to worry about their future freedom.

Government corruption has become a major public issue in the 1980s. Several scandals involving bribery and misuse of funds have surfaced, and Mahathir has pledged to clean up Malaysia's government. In the first five years of his administration, the Anti-Corruption Agency found 973 government officials guilty of illegal practices.

In October 1987 Mahathir claimed that ethnic clashes were threatening to become violent, and he arrested more than 100 political opponents. He also closed three major newspapers and banned all public gatherings. Although the moves drew international criticism, Mahathir silenced internal dissent even further by passing a harsh censorship law.

Governmental Structure

Since 1957, Malaysia has operated according to a federal system, which allows each state to retain authority over some local affairs and which gives the federal government power in national matters. When Sarawak and Sabah joined the federation in 1963, they insisted on greater control in decisions about immigration and language. An amendment to the constitution extended their rights in these areas.

Malaysia is a constitutional monarchy, which means its ruler has inherited power that is modified by a constitution. Although nine of the Malaysian states have ruling monarchs—called sultans—no nationwide monarchy existed when the federation began. But the constitution established that every five years the sultans would meet to choose one from among the

The *Yang di-Pertuan Agong* (the king elected periodically from among the sultans), Mahmood Iskandar Ibni Sultan Ismail, wears the many ceremonial decorations of his position.

nine rulers to reign as king of Malaysia until their next meeting. This temporary king, called the *Yang di-Pertuan Agong*, fills a role in the government that is mostly ceremonial.

A sultan—or a governor in those states that have no sultan—is the head of each state and wields political influence. Most power rests with the state's elected legislative assembly. At the federal level, power resides in Parliament and in the cabinet.

The national legislature consists of two houses, the Dewan Rakyat and the Dewan Negara. The members of the Dewan Rakyat are elected directly by the people of Malaysia and do most of the legislative work. The members of the Dewan Negara are appointed—some by the state legislatures, and some by the Yang di-Pertuan Agong—and function as advisers and honorary representatives.

The prime minister is the most powerful person in the Malaysian government. Whoever is the president of the majority political party in the Dewan Rakyat automatically becomes the prime minister.

The prime minister advises the Yang di-Pertuan Agong in making appointments to a seven-member supreme court, Malaysia's highest judicial body. The supreme court hears appeals from two high courts, one in Peninsular Malaysia and the other alternating between Sabah and Sarawak. A lower-court judge and jury try capital cases (for which the punishment may be execution) and kidnappings. Other criminal and civil cases are heard only by a judge.

Parliament House, with its 250-foot-tall office tower rising near Kuala Lumpur's Lake Gardens, became the seat of Malaysia's federal legislature in 1963. Both the Dewan Rakyat and the Dewan Negara – the two houses of Parliament – meet in this government complex.

Datuk Sri Dr. Mahathir Mohamad became Malaysia's prime minister in 1981. Mahathir seeks to balance Islamic fundamentalist demands with the concerns of other religious groups.

41

Malay boys light sparklers to celebrate Hari Raya Puasa, the most important Muslim holiday in Malaysia. The first day of the festival marks the end of Ramadan, which is a holy month in the Muslim calendar.

3) The People

With a land area of 127,580 square miles and a population of over 16 million, Malaysia has ample room for its population. In fact, its population density—126 people per square mile—is one of the lowest in Southeast Asia. Unlike neighboring nations, Malaysia has encouraged a slightly faster population growth rate by giving a tax advantage to large families. With its new policy, the Malaysian government hopes the number of Malaysians will increase to 70 million by the end of the twenty-first century.

Ethnic Mixture

For a small country, Malaysia has a wide diversity of peoples living within its boundaries. The nation's three largest ethnic groups are the Malays, the Chinese, and the Indians. These different groups have developed a system of parallel cultures that celebrate their own holidays, that speak their own languages, and that even pursue certain traditional occupations.

The continuing special benefits that bumiputras receive divide them from the other ethnic groups. (Bumiputras are Malaysians who belong to ethnic groups that predate the arrival of Indian, Chinese, or European immigrants.) Nevertheless, the government has tried to promote a shared national identity. The administration declared certain ethnic holidays—Chinese New Year, Indian Dewali (the Hindu Festival of Lights), Malay Hari Raya Puasa (celebrated at the end of Ramadan, the Muslim month of fasting)—as national holidays. Common celebrations encourage social mixing and provide occasions for expressions of goodwill among the ethnic groups.

Malays and other bumiputras—such as the Iban, the Bidayuh, and the Kadazan—make up about 58 percent of the population. The Chinese are the second largest ethnic group, totaling approximately 32 percent, and Indians make up roughly 8 percent of the nation's people.

MALAYS

The Malays are primarily farmers and fishermen who live in kampongs near rivers or streams. Most Malays make their homes along Peninsular Malaysia's eastern coast—in the states of Kelantan and Trengganu—and in the northern states of Kedah and Perlis.

Farming rice fields, working on small rubber plantations, and fishing in the rivers or along the coasts are still the major occupations of most Malays. Despite modernization, Malaysia's cities have not attracted large numbers of Malays. The government's NEP has created a number of government jobs—many of which are reserved for Malays—in the hope of encouraging more Malays to move to the cities, where they could take a bigger part in Malaysia's economic life.

According to official regulations, anyone who is not Muslim cannot be considered a Malay. With the rise in fundamentalism among Muslims, many Malay women have come under pressure to wear veils and full-length coverings, according to the Islamic custom requiring female modesty. Although some Muslim leaders have urged women to quit their jobs and stay at home, Malay women remain active in politics and occupy many responsible jobs in the business world.

CHINESE

Chinese Malaysians are often business-people and shopkeepers, and they hold

Courtesy of Tourist Development Corporation of Malaysia

Wayang Kulit (theater of skin) puppets are made of paper-coated buffalo hide. They are distinctly painted so the puppet master can quickly identify the one that is needed. The audience sees only the puppet's shadow cast on a screen.

Photo by L. J. Zwier

A group in Kelantan plays music on *kertoks,* a kind of one-toned percussion instrument.

many prominent positions in commerce and industry. Most Chinese Malaysians are descendants of the large wave of immigrants who came from China in the late nineteenth and early twentieth centuries, when tin mining became a major industry.

At the center of Chinese life is the extended family. The family forms the basis of the business community, and supplies, credit, and employment opportunities are distributed among family members. Malaysian Chinese speak several dialects, but Cantonese (which originated in the city of Canton, China) is commonly spoken at large gatherings.

INDIANS

The majority of Malaysia's Indian community come from the southeastern Indian state of Tamil Nadu. A need for rubber-estate workers during the first three decades of the twentieth century brought many Indian immigrants to Malaysia in order to do manual labor. Since then, however, Indians have become active in trade and commerce, and they make up a large share of the work force on the Malaysian railway system. Other Indian Malaysians work in the nation's banking and investment industries. Most Malaysian Indians speak Tamil, a language of southern India.

Other Ethnic Groups

Besides Malays, bumiputras include many other groups. In Peninsular Malaysia, these peoples are generally known as the *Orang Asli* (original people), but they are not a unified ethnic community. Most of

A trishaw—a three-wheeled, pedal-powered taxicab—passes by a row of Chinese shops in Penang.

Tamil rubber workers, originally from southeastern India, bring their day's load of latex to the collecting shed. A weak acid will be added to the mixture in a nearby factory, causing the latex to form a white, elastic mass—rubber.

In a Bidayuh village in Sarawak a bumiputra woman strings nipa palm leaves on a pole. The completed pole will form part of an atap (thatched) roof.

the Orang Asli traditionally live as hunters and gatherers in the deep jungles of the peninsula. Many of them supplement their livelihoods with small-scale agriculture—such as planting mountain rice—but large permanent settlements are not part of the Orang Asli way of life. Government efforts to extend health care, education, and other social services to the Orang Asli have encouraged some of them to break with tradition and to settle in permanent villages.

On the island of Borneo, several dozen original ethnic groups populate the mountains. The most numerous are the Iban, who make up about 30 percent of the population of Sarawak. Many Iban have taken jobs with the oil companies that operate in eastern Sarawak, and some have moved to Kuching, Bintalu, and other cities.

Most Iban, however, still live in the untamed interior of the island in large communal dwellings (called longhouses) that usually shelter about 20 families. The Iban,

High in minarets all over Malaysia, muezzins (Muslim criers) call the faithful to prayer five times each day.

like most of the other Bornean peoples, plant mountain rice, gather jungle vegetables, and raise chickens and pigs. To earn cash for the articles they cannot produce themselves—such as salt and medicine—the Iban grow pepper and cassavas (starchy, edible roots).

Religion

Although Malaysia's constitution guarantees freedom of religion, Islam is the country's official faith. Islam began during the seventh century A.D. in Arabia. A prophet named Muhammad received messages from Allah (the Islamic name for God) that now form the basis of Islam.

Five main duties fall upon Muslims—having faith in Allah, praying five times a day, giving to the poor, fasting during the holy month of Ramadan, and making a pilgrimage to Mecca (Islam's holiest city, located in Saudi Arabia). Although Muslims are free to convert others to Is-

Malay fishermen breakfast on grilled squid, before going to work with their nets. White skullcaps mark their wearers as hajis—Muslims who have made the pilgrimage (hajj) to Mecca.

The needlelike minaret in the center, nearly 250 feet tall, belongs to the National Mosque in Kuala Lumpur.

lam, in most of Malaysia it is illegal to attempt to convert a Muslim to another religion.

In addition to the large number of Malay Muslims, a few Indian and Chinese people also follow Islam. Mosques (Muslim places of worship) are well attended, and during the month of Ramadan faithful Muslims neither eat nor drink from dawn to dusk. Malaysian Muslims often save money for years to fund the hajj (pilgrimage) to Mecca. Pilgrims who return from the hajj are treated with great respect within the Muslim community.

Besides following the Islamic way of life, Muslims also must follow Islamic law. Muslim religious authorities in Malaysia may arrest, fine, physically punish, and jail Muslims for violating religious laws, even if they have broken no civil laws.

A small minority of Chinese are Christians, but most Chinese follow the religions of Confucianism, Daoism (also known as Taoism), or Buddhism, sometimes blending the elements of these religions. Confucianism focuses on practical wisdom and order in family and social life. Daoism leads believers to follow the Dao (the Way) to achieve personal freedom. Liberation from suffering by living a life of detachment from worldly things is Buddhism's goal. Many Chinese also revere their ancestors as part of their religious observance, making a family shrine out of pictures or belongings of deceased parents or grandparents.

Most of Malaysia's Indians are Hindus. Unlike Christianity and Islam, which are monotheistic (one-god) religions, followers of Hinduism worship many gods. Hindus dedicate their temples to a protector god who watches over believers, helps them to work the land, and keeps their families safe. Hinduism has many rituals, although few are necessary for following the Hindu way of life.

The Indian population also includes a small percentage of Christians, Muslims, Sikhs (followers of a religion that developed from Hinduism and Islam), and Parsis. Parsis follow Zoroastrianism, a religion

Christ Church was built by the Dutch in 1753 of pink brick from Zeeland in the Netherlands. The Church stands near Malacca's Stadthuys, the Dutch town hall built in 1641, and is a reminder of early European colonial influence.

Buddhists from all over Southeast Asia contributed money to build this pagoda (temple) and other buildings of the Kek-Lok-Si monastery and temple on Penang Island. The first tier of the tower is dedicated to Kwan Yin, the Chinese goddess of mercy.

Independent Picture Service

founded in the sixth century B.C. by Zoroaster.

On Borneo many of the original ethnic groups are animists—that is, they believe that all living and nonliving things have a spirit and that religious activities can make the spirits friendly to the believers. A large number of the Bornean peoples are Christian and belong mostly to the Anglican, Roman Catholic, or Methodist churches.

Language

The official language of Malaysia is *Bahasa Malaysia,* or Malay, which belongs to the Malayo-Polynesian family of languages and is related to many tongues of the South Pacific. Bahasa Malaysia and *Bahasa Indonesia,* the official speech of Indonesia, are different dialects of Malay, and speakers of one can easily understand speakers of the other. Malay has borrowed many words from Sanskrit, Arabic, and English.

At the time of independence, many non-Malays objected to making Malay the nation's official language, claiming that English would be a better compromise. The government, however, decided to choose a language that was not a reminder of its colonial past and that was easy to learn.

By the 1980s non-Malays had begun to accept the Malay language, but its use was not universal in Malaysia. In addition to the peoples of the Sarawak and Sabah jungles, who have little contact with speakers of Bahasa Malaysia, many Chinese Malaysians speak little or no Malay. Resentment continues over the official status of Bahasa Malaysia, and some non-Malays refuse to use the language—even though they know it—in conversation with other non-Malays.

48

English, the official language used during the colonial period, is widely spoken in Malaysia, and a number of urban Malaysians of Chinese or Indian descent speak it as their primary language. Besides learning English as a subject in school, Malaysians have a great deal of exposure to the language from U.S., British, and Australian programs that regularly appear on Malaysian television.

Education

The Malaysian educational system follows the model installed by the British during colonial rule. At about the age of six, a child begins primary school, which may be taught in Bahasa Malaysia, Chinese, or Tamil, depending on the language of the students. Each year of school is called a standard, so a standard four student is in the fourth year of primary school.

At about the age of 12, students attend lower secondary school, which is taught in Bahasa Malaysia and which lasts for three years. Each year of secondary school is called a form. Students progress through the forms by passing tests in areas such as art, science, technical topics, or vocational subjects, in which they choose to specialize during the upper forms.

Malaysia has six national universities, three of which give master's degrees and doctorates as well as undergraduate degrees. The oldest and best known is the University of Malaya which is located in Kuala Lumpur and includes a medical school and a law school. Although the Malaysian government sponsors the overseas education of many Malaysians, almost all national and overseas scholarships are reserved for bumiputras.

Malaysia has a well-educated society, despite the fact that some of its regions are isolated and hard to reach. About 95 percent of Malaysian children of primary-school age are enrolled in classes. As a result, 81 percent of Malaysian men and 60 percent of Malaysian women can read and write.

Courtesy of UNICEF

These primary school students are taught in the official language of Malaysia—*Bahasa Malaysia.* Other ethnic groups learn in Chinese or Tamil, and Malaysian secondary students also learn English in school.

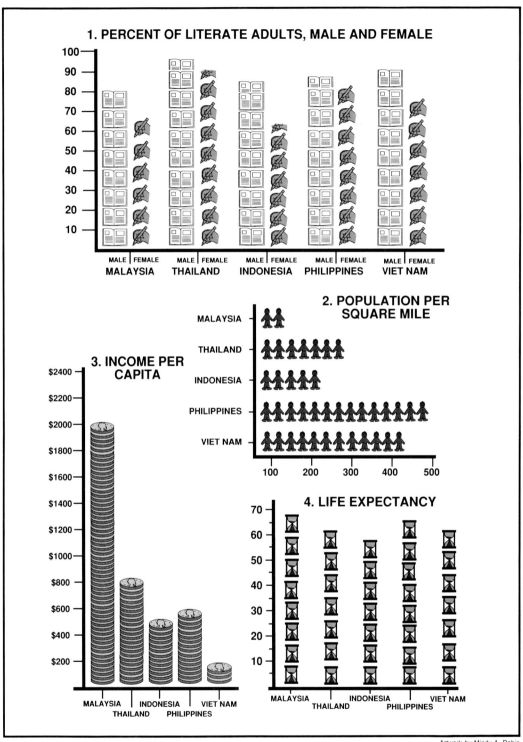

1. PERCENT OF LITERATE ADULTS, MALE AND FEMALE

	MALE	FEMALE	MALE	FEMALE	MALE	FEMALE	MALE	FEMALE	MALE	FEMALE
	MALAYSIA		THAILAND		INDONESIA		PHILIPPINES		VIET NAM	

2. POPULATION PER SQUARE MILE

MALAYSIA
THAILAND
INDONESIA
PHILIPPINES
VIET NAM

100   200   300   400   500

3. INCOME PER CAPITA

$2400
$2200
$2000
$1800
$1600
$1400
$1200
$1000
$800
$600
$400
$200

MALAYSIA   INDONESIA   VIET NAM
THAILAND   PHILIPPINES

4. LIFE EXPECTANCY

70
60
50
40
30
20
10

MALAYSIA   INDONESIA   VIET NAM
THAILAND   PHILIPPINES

Artwork by Mindy A. Rabin

Depicted in this chart are factors relating to the standard of living in five countries in southeastern Asia. Information taken from "1987 World Population Data Sheet," "The World's Women: A Profile," and "Children of the World" compiled by the Population Reference Bureau, Washington, D.C.

The Arts

Many of the traditional arts of Malaysia
—batik, for example—are made with cloth.
To create a batik design, an artist paints
or presses a wax design onto a piece of
fabric, then dips the fabric into colored
dye. The color will soak into the cloth ev-
erywhere except where the wax remains.
The artist then scrapes off the wax, presses
new wax designs onto the cloth, and dips
it into a different dye. By repeating this
several times, a batik artist blends colors
and designs on the cloth.

Malaysians also excel in the art of weav-
ing. Especially in the states of Kelantan
and Trengganu, weavers produce elaborate *kain songket*—fabrics in which gold
or silver threads form geometric designs—
on looms in the home.

Other arts that distinguish Malaysia
are created from the raw materials that are
abundant in the country. The Orang Asli
of the peninsula carve hardwoods into ex-
pressive figures of animals and super-
natural beings. Wood carving is also a
highly developed art among the people of

Kain songket (fabric) often features intricate symmetrical
patterns of gold- or silver-colored thread. Some kain
songket cloth contains real silver or gold, which is hand-
woven into the design.

Sarawak, who are famous for detailed,
abstract representations of the hornbill
bird. Metalworking has long been a special
craft of the people of the tin-rich peninsula,

Malay women at a government training center near Kuala Trengganu use dyed wicker to weave handbags and other goods
for tourists.

51

Photo by Bernice K. Condit

A batik factory worker presses designs in wax onto cloth that will then be dyed. The color soaks into the cloth around the wax imprints. Afterward, the wax is removed, and the process is repeated with different dyes.

and residents of Selangor and Perak make handsome pewter (a mixture of tin and lead) items.

Traditional Malaysian architecture is both functional and beautiful. The high-pitched roof of a kampong house may be covered with clay tiles, corrugated zinc, or atap (sewn panels of dried branches from the nipa palm). For decoration, the house may have elaborate wooden grillwork under its eaves and an ornately tiled set of stairs leading to its front door. Perhaps the most dramatic decorative touch applied to some larger, traditional buildings is a Minangkabau roof that flares upward at both ends and resembles oxhorns. This style originated in the Minangkabau Valley of Sumatra.

Much of the music that Malaysians enjoy is imported from the United States, Great Britain, and elsewhere. Rock and popular music exist in spite of the objections of some Muslim fundamentalists who believe that Western music is a dangerous influence. Both Malay and non-Malay singers perform in the nation's many nightclubs and appear on local television. Perhaps the most unusual traditional music in Malaysia comes from Sarawak, where musicians play the guitar-like *sape*—as well as gongs, drums, and bamboo flutes—to produce a highly rhythmic sound.

Health

The quality of health care in Malaysia has increased substantially within the last

Independent Picture Service

Malaysian women wear rich kain songket garments for a performance of traditional dances.

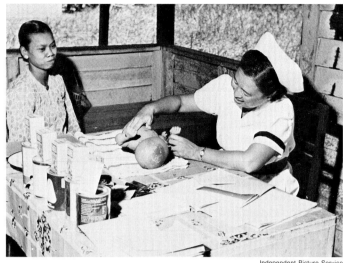

A nurse at a government clinic examines an infant, as its mother sits nearby. The clinics are part of Malaysia's effort to improve health care in rural areas.

40 years. The improvement in health standards is due to strong governmental support of programs in nutrition and preventive medicine. The number of deaths per 1,000 people dropped from 20 in 1947 to 7 in 1987. The infant mortality rate (the number of deaths among children less than one year old) has also declined during the same period from 102 deaths per 1,000 live births to 30.

Medical personnel and hospital facilities in Malaysia are of high quality. Government efforts to control disease-carrying mosquitoes have sharply reduced the incidence of malaria, once a major ailment throughout Malaysia. As a result of these improvements, the life expectancy for people living in Malaysia is 67 years, the second highest figure in the Southeast Asian region.

Sports

Malaysians participate in a variety of sports. Some games are native to the country, and others originated in Great Britain

This Iban woman lives with her family in a Sarawak village. Because of improvement in health care, her children can expect to live to be 67 years of age.

The bow-like addition to this colorful kite from Kelantan makes a humming sound as the wind plays over the bamboo and paper.

and North America. Of Malaysian sports, *sepak takraw* (Malay football) is the best known. In this game, which is similar to a combination of volleyball and soccer, players use their feet or heads to knock a light-weight ball made of rattan (interwoven palm stems) back and forth across a net. Top spinning and kite flying are also common Malaysian pastimes.

Of the imported sports, soccer is by far the most popular. Many schools compete, and rivalries are intense. Soccer teams represent each of the Malaysian states as well as the armed forces. The teams compete annually in a regional tournament with the nations of Singapore and Brunei.

Badminton is another of Malaysia's leading sports. Malaysian teams have often won the Thomas Cup—the symbol of international badminton competition. The game remains extremely popular and, along with basketball, field hockey, and cricket, attracts many enthusiasts.

Sepak takraw combines some features of volleyball and some of soccer. The players may not touch the rattan ball with their hands or arms.

The bark of this rubber tree has been carefully scraped so that the tree's latex, the raw material for rubber, will drip into the bowl attached to the trunk. Rubber production has been a major industry in Malaysia since the end of the nineteenth century.

Courtesy of Malaysian Rubber Bureau

4) The Economy

The main activity of the Malaysian economy until the 1980s had been the production of raw materials—such as petroleum, timber, rubber, palm oil, and tin—for export. Although the income from these exports was good for many years, surpluses on world markets for almost all of these commodities have driven prices down in the 1980s. As a result, Malaysia's economy has slowed, and the nation is now taking steps to broaden its industrial base.

Petroleum

Petroleum products—crude oil and natural gas—became Malaysia's most profitable export in the late 1970s. Malaysia has two main oil-producing regions, one off the

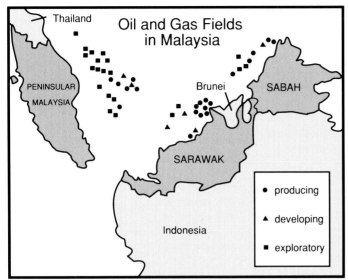

Oil produced from Malaysia's off-shore drilling platforms—shown as dots in the South China Sea—is a central part of the national economy.

Artwork by Mindy A. Rabin

coast of Sarawak and Sabah and the other off the eastern coast of Peninsular Malaysia. In both of these regions, drilling rigs must be anchored in the ocean floor to extract the petroleum.

An agency of the Malaysian government, PETRONAS supervises all exploration, drilling, and processing of petroleum products. It also decides which international firms may participate in Malaysia's oil business. In the 1980s four firms—Sarawak Shell, Sabah Shell, ESSO Production Malaysia, and Elf Aquitaine—explored for oil in Malaysia. As part of its effort to become a more industrialized country, Malaysia has built five oil refineries and other factories to process the by-products of petroleum.

Although Malaysia does not belong to the Organization of Petroleum Exporting

Petrochemical plants in Malaysia produce chemicals, such as carbon, from the by-products that result when petroleum is processed into refined oil and gasoline.

Courtesy of Ashland Oil, Inc.

Countries (OPEC)—a group that sets prices and production quotas among its members to influence the world oil market —Malaysia is affected by OPEC's decisions. In particular, OPEC's decision to establish extremely high prices for oil in the 1970s led to a large jump in Malaysia's oil earnings. But all oil producers wanted to get their product to market while the price was high. By the mid-1980s so much oil was available that the price dropped. In January 1986 a barrel of Malaysian crude oil sold for $27, but by August 1986 the price had dropped to $10.

In 1986 crude oil and natural gas accounted for almost 23 percent of Malaysia's exports and earned the country $3 billion in revenue. Malaysia ranks among the top twenty nations in the world in known reserves and probably has large undiscovered oil deposits.

Forestry

After petroleum, Malaysia's three most important exports are palm oil, timber, and rubber. Malaysia is the largest manufacturer of palm oil in the world, producing 62 percent of the world's supply.

Oil palms are stout trees that bear bunches of a reddish-brown, nutlike fruit which contain a vegetable oil used in dozens of different products. For example, palm oil is an ingredient in the manufacture of cosmetics, margarine, and even light-weight fuels and lubricants. When profits from rubber fell, many Malaysian farmers cut down their rubber trees and replanted their fields with oil palms. The price of palm oil, however, took a sharp dive in the mid-1980s because of an over-supply on the world market. This product is another upon which Malaysia may not be able to depend in the future.

With vast rain-forests, Malaysia is a storehouse of valuable timber, including tropical hardwoods such as meranti, mahogany, and belian. Especially in the states of Sarawak and Sabah, logging is

A worker uses a long pole to harvest the oil-bearing kernels growing on an oil palm.

Plantation workers tend rubber trees, periodically scraping thin layers of bark away so that the flow of latex can continue.

A Malaysian worker pours latex into containers for shipment to a rubber factory. Stations for collecting latex are positioned throughout rubber plantations.

a major business. Low prices on world markets and an increasing need to conserve forests, however, have slowed Malaysia's timber harvesting.

Although rubber is a significant export, its importance to Malaysia's economy has steadily declined since the development of synthetic (chemically made) rubber. In 1970 rubber accounted for about 22 percent of Malaysia's export earnings, but by 1986 it contributed less than 10 percent. Compared to prices of some of Malaysia's other export products, the price of rubber has been stable throughout the mid-1980s. The amount of rubber Malaysia exports has also stayed relatively constant.

Raw latex is strained and formed into continuous sheets, which are broken up into chunks to promote thorough drying. Here, a laborer readies chunks in bins for the drying process.

58

After drying, the rubber chunks pass through a compactor that presses them into bales. Thirty bales, which together weigh a ton, are packed together for shipment.

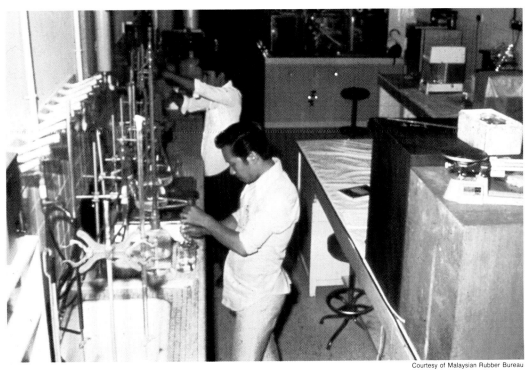

Technicians test the quality of recently produced rubber in a laboratory at a rubber factory. Samples are sliced from random bales as they exit the compactor.

Moving across the ore-bearing soil, huge dredges scoop up earth and separate tin ore from gravel and sand.

A farmer on a motorized plow chugs slowly through a wet rice paddy. Mechanization has been gradually introduced to Malaysian agriculture.

Although some progress has been made toward developing higher-yielding rubber trees to compete with synthetic rubber, growing natural rubber is no longer the high-profit business it once was. Now a large percentage of Malaysia's rubber production—about 61 percent—is in the hands of small-scale landholders who each own less than 25 acres of rubber trees.

Mining

Once the most important natural resource on the Malay Peninsula, tin is now a less significant part of Malaysia's economy. In 1986 tin accounted for only 1.6 percent of the nation's export earnings. The world-wide tin trade became so unpredictable in the mid-1980s that the London and Kuala Lumpur tin markets closed for more than four months in an attempt to calm the trading atmosphere. Tin mining continues, however, especially in the states of Selangor and Perak. Tin dredges (earth-scooping machines) operate in Malaysia's large open-pit mines, and many other small mines are in operation as well.

Peninsular Malaysia also mines iron and bauxite (the raw material for making aluminum), and Sabah has a copper mine. These minerals, however, do not play a major part in Malaysia's economy. Other mineral resources that exist in small amounts are coal, antimony (a brittle metal used in alloys), and gold.

Agriculture

Because over 60 percent of its population lives in rural areas, Malaysia has been working to improve its agricultural economy. Government agencies have sponsored improvements that include large irrigation and drainage systems, new farm machinery (especially power tillers), and breeds of crops that produce higher yields.

Although Malaysia's rice yield per acre is as high as any in Southeast Asia, the country does not grow enough of the grain

Courtesy of Tourist Development Corporation of Malaysia

Malaysia's pepper supply starts as small green berries on pepper plants. The crop darkens as the berries dry in the Sarawak sun.

put to make tires, shoes, medical supplies, and other manufactured goods. Still the world's leading source of raw rubber, Malaysia furnishes about 31.5 percent of the world's total. The country hopes to become one of the largest suppliers of rubber products as well.

Perhaps most notable in Malaysia's industrial expansion is its entry into the automobile business. In the early 1980s the Malaysian government invited the Japanese automaker Mitsubishi to set up an automobile factory in Malaysia. Cars are assembled in Malaysia with primarily Japanese-made parts. The model known as the Proton Saga went into production in 1985 and has been sold successfully in Malaysia. The government plans to export the Saga to New Zealand, the United States, and other countries.

to feed a population that eats it as a staple food. Consequently, rice must be imported from Thailand and Burma. If Malaysia chose to use its land for more crops for domestic consumption, it could feed its people, but so far the country has decided to plant money-making export crops and to import much of its food.

Malaysia's export crops include pineapples, coconuts, tea, coffee, and cassavas (from which tapioca is produced). Sarawak produces a large proportion of the world's supply of pepper. Grown on small plots, pepper bushes produce small, green berries that are dried in the sun until they become hard peppercorns.

Industry

Because prices for its raw materials have often fallen, Malaysia has decided to broaden its industrial economy. The nation's plan is to develop many industries so that sudden price drops for a single commodity will not significantly damage the national economy.

Malaysia is developing a rubber-products industry that uses its own rubber out-

Independent Picture Service

A vital import and export trade keeps Malaysia's dock workers busy in Selangor.

Hilly Penang Island is served by a funicular railway—one in which the cars are pulled by a cable instead of being powered by an onboard engine.

Transportation and Energy

Malaysia maintains a high-quality system of roads, electrical power lines, telephone networks, and other basic services. The main road that links the major cities of the western coastal plain is the North-South Highway, which is being enlarged into four-lanes. Another major project is the construction of the Pan-Borneo Highway, intended eventually to run the length of Sarawak, to cross Brunei, and to reach the northern tip of Sabah. Presently, Sarawak has paved roads only in and near its larger cities.

The railway system in Peninsular Malaysia dates from 1931. Branch lines from the east and west join, becoming a single track as they approach the tip of the peninsula. Sabah has a rail service that extends southward from Kota Kinabalu, but Sarawak has no railway. Flights of the government-owned Malaysian Airline System link these Bornean states to the rest of the nation and provide Malaysia with an international air network as well.

Electricity from hydroelectric and gas-burning plants reaches almost every settlement in Peninsular Malaysia as well as the cities of the Bornean states. Malaysia's public utilities are among the best in Asia, and most Malaysians enjoy basic services that are uncommon throughout much of the world.

Tourism

Malaysia is a popular destination for tourists from Singapore, Australia, and Japan, and the country's tourist industry is growing rapidly. With natural beauty, excellent public services, and a largely English-speaking population, Malaysia has the potential to become a vacation spot for both North Americans and Europeans.

As part of the country's effort to attract North Americans, the Malaysian Airline System introduced direct flights to the west coast of the United States in 1986. Through its Tourist Develoment Corporation, Malaysia promotes itself as a destination for jungle safaris, river trips, and mountain treks.

Future Challenges

Malaysia's continued growth as an industrialized nation depends partly on how it handles the economic challenges it faces. Fluctuating prices and a shrinking demand for its raw materials have prompted Malaysia to expand the industrial sector of its economy. By developing petroleum processing plants, new rubber goods, and an automobile industry, Malaysia hopes to increase its economic growth.

Solving the conflict between the Malays, the Chinese, and the Indians over bumiputra special privileges has an economic as well as a social aspect. Some nonbumiputras are beginning to seek opportunities elsewhere by emigrating from Malaysia to

A tourist takes advantage of the Malaysian weather and the nation's excellent beaches.

and talented businesspeople if tensions over government policies that favor bumiputras are not eased.

The increasing power of Muslim fundamentalists also concerns the non-Muslim Chinese and Indian communities in Malaysia. In an already highly splintered national population, the goals of Muslims who are working for an Islamic state further separate Malaysians from one another. Prime Minister Mahathir's political leadership has so far allowed for advances in Islamic influence without upsetting the balance of other interests.

Malaysia has a history of tension caused by separate ethnic communities and by uneven distribution of wealth. But a willingness to compromise and to accommodate also forms part of the country's national identity. If economic difficulties at the end of the twentieth century do not increase, Malaysians may find ways to grow prosperous together.

countries that do not discriminate against people because of their ethnic origin. Malaysia may thus lose many skilled workers

The assembly plant for the Proton Saga automobile is a cooperative venture between Mitsubishi Motors Corporation of Japan and the Malaysian government. The joint effort exemplifies the desire of the national leadership to broaden the range of the country's manufactured goods.

Index

Abdullah, Sultan, 28
Agriculture, 10, 25, 30, 43-46, 57, 60-61.
The Alliance, 34, 37-38
Anwar Ibrahim, 39
Architecture, 21, 23, 41, 46-48, 52
Arts and crafts, 51-52, 54
Automobile industry, 61-63
Aviation, 31, 62
Bahasa Malaysia, 48-49
Barisan Nasional (the National Front), 38
Bidayuh, 43, 45
Birch, W. W., 28
Borneo, 5, 8-9, 11, 13, 16-17, 26-27, 36, 45-46, 48, 56, 62
Briggs Plan, 32
British East India Company, 25
British North Borneo Company, 26-27
Brooke, Charles, 26-27
Brooke, Charles Vyner, 27
Brooke, James, 26
Brunei, 8, 26-27, 35, 54, 62
Bumiputras, 35-38, 42-45, 49, 62-63
Burma, 9, 11, 34, 61
Cassavas, 46, 61
Celebes Sea, 11
Chenderoh, Lake, 13
China, 2, 6, 20-23, 28, 31, 44
immigrants from, 6, 22-23, 26-28, 30-38, 42-44, 47-49, 62-63
Cities, 18-19
Climate, 10, 12-15, 28, 63
Clothing, 2, 35, 37, 40, 43, 46, 52
Communications, 7, 13, 30, 39, 49, 52, 62
Communism, 7, 30-34
Communist guerrillas, 31-34
Constitutional monarchy, 39-40
Constitutions, 34-35, 39, 46
Dewan Negara, 40-41
Dewan Rakyat, 40-41
Drugs, illegal, 38
Eastern coastal plain, 5, 10, 14, 43, 56
Economy, 6-7, 10, 30, 35-36, 38, 43, 55-63
Education, 30, 35, 39, 45, 49, 54
Elections, 7, 34, 37
The Emergency, 32-34
Energy and fuels, 13, 34, 55-57, 62
Exports, 7, 10, 30, 55, 57-58, 60-61
Federated Malay States, 28-29
Fishing, 10, 23, 25, 43, 46
Flora and fauna, 8, 10, 14-18, 45, 52, 57
Food, 33, 46, 61
Foreign companies, 7, 56
Free ports, 18, 25
Gautama Buddha, 21
George Town, 6, 18, 25
Government
bumiputras' special privileges, 7, 30, 35-38, 42, 49, 62-63
corruption and repression, 7, 38-39
economic and social programs, 38, 42, 45, 53, 56, 63
Islam's role in, 23-24, 26, 28, 31, 38-39, 41, 46-47, 63
stability, 30-31, 34, 38
structure, 31, 39-41

Great Britain, 6, 18, 25-29, 31-47, 49, 52-53, 60
Health and diseases, 28, 33-34, 45-46, 49, 52-53
Hinduism, 21, 23, 42, 47
History, 20-39
British colonial rule, 6, 18, 25-32, 34, 36, 48-49
early settlers, 20-24, 46, 48
European influence, 18, 24-26, 47
independence, 5, 7, 20, 31-39, 48
Holidays and festivals, 20, 34-35, 42-43, 46-47
Housing, 32-34, 38, 45, 52
Hydroelectricity, 13, 62
Iban, 26, 35, 43, 45-46, 53
Imports, 61
India, 6, 21, 23-25, 30, 44-45
immigrants from, 6, 21, 23, 30-31, 34-37, 42-45, 47, 49, 62-63
Indonesia, Republic of, 16-17, 21, 36, 48
Industry, 6-7, 30, 44-45, 52, 55-59, 61-63
Ipoh, 18, 32
Islam, 23-24, 26, 28, 30-31, 35, 37-39, 41-43, 46-47, 63
Japan, 5, 27, 31, 34, 62-63
Jungles, 15-17, 20, 32, 36, 45-46, 48, 62
Kadazan, 35, 43
Kain songket, 51-52
Kampongs, 13, 21, 25, 43, 52
Kapas Island, 14
Kapit, 13
Kedah, 28, 34, 43
Kelantan, 28, 43, 51, 54
Kinabalu, 26
Kota Kinabalu, 14, 18, 62
Kuala Lumpur, 10, 14, 18-19, 27, 34, 37-39, 41, 47, 49, 60
Kuching, 14, 18-19, 26, 45
Languages, 18-19, 21, 39, 42, 44, 48-49, 62
Latex, 30, 45, 55, 57-58
Lee Kuan Yew, 35-36
Literacy, 49
Livestock, 46
Low, Sir Hugh, 28
Mahathir Mohamad, Datuk Sri Dr., 38-39, 41, 63
Mahmood Iskandar Ibni Sultan Ismail, 40
Majapahit (Javanese kingdom), 22
Malacca, 23-26, 31, 47
Malaya, Federation of, 32, 34-35, 37
Malayan Chinese Association (MCA), 34, 38
Malayan Indian Congress (MIC), 34, 38
Malayan Union, 32
Malay People's Anti-Japanese Army (MPAJA), 31-32
Malays (people), 6-7, 13, 18, 20-21, 23, 25, 28, 30-32, 35-38, 42-43, 46-48, 52, 62
Malaysia, Federation of, 7-8, 35-36, 39
boundaries, size, and location, 5, 8-9, 35, 42
flags, 20, 32, 34, 39
names of, 8, 25, 28-29, 32, 34-37

Maps and charts, 4, 9, 12, 29, 50, 56
Mecca, 46-47
Military, 18, 24-26, 31-33, 36, 54
Mining, 18, 27-28, 30, 60
Monsoons, 10, 12-14
Mountains and hills, 9-11, 13-14, 62
Muhammad, 23, 46
Music, 2, 43, 52
Muzaffar Shah, 23-24
Natural resources, 5, 7, 51, 55, 60-62
Negri Sembilan, 28
Netherlands, 25-26, 47
New Economic Policy (NEP), 38, 43
Nonbumiputras, 35-38, 62
North America, 54, 62
North-South Highway, 62
Orang Asli (original people), 44-45, 51
Organization of Petroleum Exporting Countries (OPEC), 56-57
Palm oil, 10, 55, 57
Pan-Borneo Highway, 62
Pangkor, Treaty of, 28
Paramesvara, 23
Parliament, 34, 37-38, 40-41
Parliament House, 37, 41
Parti Islam Se-Malaysia (PAS), 38
Penang Island, 6, 18, 25, 44, 48, 62
Peng, Chin, 34
Peninsular Malaysia. 5, 8-11, 13-14, 16, 18, 22-24, 26-32, 34-36, 40, 43-45, 51-52, 56, 60, 62
People, 42-54
customs and cultural identity, 3, 21, 28, 35, 37, 42-43, 46, 63
ethnic groups and conflicts, 6-7, 18, 20-21, 23, 28, 30-32, 34-39, 42-49, 62-63
immigrants, 6, 20-23, 28, 30, 32, 35, 39, 44
lifestyles, 2, 18, 32-34, 43-45, 47, 49, 51-53, 60
occupations, 28, 30, 32-33, 35, 43-46, 51-52, 57-59, 61
standard of living, 5-6, 30, 32, 34, 50, 53, 62
Pepper and other spices, 24-25, 46, 61
Perak, 28, 52, 60
Perlis, 28, 43
Petroleum and oil, 45, 55-57, 62
PETRONAS, 56
Philippines, 7, 20, 36
Pirates, 23, 26, 28
Plantations, 30, 32, 43-44, 47-48
Political parties, 34, 37-38
Population, 5, 10, 18, 20, 30, 35-36, 42-43, 45, 60
Ports, 6, 18, 23, 25, 61
Portugal, 24-25, 31
Precipitation, 10, 12-14
Prime ministers, 34, 36-38, 40-41, 63
Raffles, Thomas Stamford, 25
Railways, 28, 30, 44, 62
Rain-forests, 10, 13-14, 26-27, 57-58. *See also* Timber
Rajas, 26-27
Ramadan, 42-43, 46-47

Religion, 21-24, 26, 28, 31, 35, 38-39, 41-43, 46-48, 63
Rice, 2, 11, 43, 45-46, 60-61
Rivers and streams, 11, 13-14, 17-19, 21, 27, 43, 62
Roads, 13, 30, 62
Rubber, 6, 10, 30, 32, 43-45, 55, 57-62
Sabah, 7-9, 11, 13-14, 16, 18, 26-27, 32, 35-36, 39-40, 48, 56-57, 60, 62
Sarawak, 8-9, 11, 13-14, 16-20, 26-27, 32, 35-36, 39-40, 45, 48, 51-53, 56-57, 61-62
Selangor, 28, 52, 60-61
Sepak takraw, 53
Shipping, 13, 18-19, 21-22, 61
Sibu, 13, 18
Singapore, 5, 8, 16, 23, 25, 32, 35-36, 54, 62
South China Sea, 5, 9-10, 13-14, 18, 56
Southeast Asia, 5, 8, 11, 21, 25, 30, 42, 48, 53, 60
Sports and recreation, 52-54
Sri Vijaya (Buddhist kingdom), 22
Straits Settlements, 25, 27-29
Sukarno, 36
Sukhothai (Thai kingdom), 22
Sultans, 24-28, 32, 39-40
Sulu, 27
Sulu Sea, 11, 18
Sumatra, 16, 21-23, 52
Sumatran, 13-14
Supreme court, 40
Swamps, 10-11, 13
Tahan, Mount, 10
Tai Zong, 22
Tamil (people), 44-45
Tapir, 16-17
Temples and mosques, 21, 23, 28, 46-48
Thailand, 8, 10, 22-23, 28-29, 61
Timber, 26-27, 55, 57-58
Tin, 6, 18, 27-28, 30, 51-52, 55, 60
Tourism, 51, 62
Trade and commerce, 6-7, 13, 18, 21-28, 30, 35, 44, 46, 57, 61
Transportation, 13, 19, 22, 28, 30, 44, 61-62
Treaties and agreements, 25-28, 32, 36
Trengganu, 5, 28, 43, 51
Tumasik, 23
Tun Abdul Razak, 38
Tunku Abdul Rahman, 20, 34-38
United East India Company, 25
United Malays National Organization (UMNO), 34, 38
United Nations, 7
United States, 49, 52, 61-62
Wars and armed conflicts, 7, 22, 24, 26-28, 31-34, 36-38. *See also* Communist guerrillas; Military; World War II
Western coastal plain, 6, 10, 13-14, 18, 21, 23-24, 27-28, 62
World War II, 26-27, 31-32
Yang di-Pertuan Agong, 40